B IS FOR BUNNY

A SPRINGTIME ALPHABET BOOK

For Jake and Liza, my little puddle-jumpers!—T.L.S.

To Fran Gaurang, thanks for all of your support!—S.R.

PRICE STERN SLOAN
Published by the Penguin Group
Penguin Group (USA) Inc., 375 Hudson Street, New York, New York 10014, U.S.A.
Penguin Group (Canada), 90 Eglinton Avenue East, Suite 700, Toronto, Ontario, Canada M4P 2Y3
(a division of Pearson Penguin Canada Inc.)
Penguin Books Ltd, 80 Strand, London WC2R 0RL, England
Penguin Ireland, 25 St Stephen's Green, Dublin 2, Ireland
(a division of Penguin Books Ltd)
Penguin Group (Australia), 250 Camberwell Road, Camberwell, Victoria 3124, Australia
(a division of Pearson Australia Group Pty Ltd)
Penguin Books India Pvt Ltd, 11 Community Centre, Panchsheel Park, New Delhi - 110 017, India
Penguin Group (NZ), Cnr Airborne and Rosedale Roads, Albany, Auckland 1310, New Zealand
(a division of Pearson New Zealand Ltd)
Penguin Books (South Africa) (Pty) Ltd, 24 Sturdee Avenue, Rosebank, Johannesburg 2196, South Africa

Penguin Books Ltd, Registered Offices:
80 Strand, London WC2R 0RL, England

Library of Congress Control Number: 2005013262

ISBN 0-8431-1826-1   10 9 8 7 6 5 4 3 2

B IS FOR BUNNY

A SPRINGTIME ALPHABET BOOK

By Tanya Lee Stone

ILLUSTRATED by Sue Ramá

PSS!

PRICE STERN SLOAN

A is for announcement

Let's shout out a cheer,
'Cause we think that spring
Is the best time of year!

B is for bunny

She's always hip-hopping,
Her button nose twitching,
Her long ears flip-flopping!

C is for caterpillar

It inched up a tree,
Then climbed on my finger—
It's tickling me!

D is for daffodils

Sunny and bright.
They've popped up all over—
A perfect spring sight!

E is for Earth Day

We have to be smart,
And care for our planet,
So please do your part!

F is for farmyard

Where little foals neigh,
While piglets and lambs
Lie asleep in the hay!

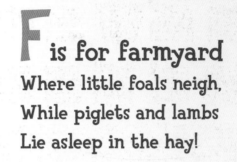

G is for grass

Cropping up fresh and new.
Can't wait to go barefoot
Run through it with you!

H is for hatch

From an egg comes a chick—
It pecks with its beak,
And its tiny legs kick!

I is for insects
Creep-crawling on by.
The ones that have wings
Go bizz-buzz as they fly!

J is for jump rope

I bounce and I hop.
The rope keeps on twirling—
I don't want to stop!

K is for Kite

Flying high in the air
Diving and climbing
And soaring up there!

L is for ladybugs

Spotted and round.
They travel in groups.
Look how many I found!

M is for mud

We love squishing through muck.
It's plenty of fun,
But watch out—don't get stuck!

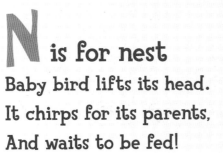**N** is for nest

Baby bird lifts its head.
It chirps for its parents,
And waits to be fed!

O is for outside

We drink from the fountain,
We swing on the swings,
And play King-of-the-mountain!

P is for puddles

We splash through each one.
We stomp and we giggle—
There's nothing more fun!

Q is for quacking

Eight ducks waddle past.
They follow their mother—
The little one's last!

R is for rainbow

Spray-painting the sky.
I wish I could touch it
It's up way too high!

S is for seeds

Sprouting up in neat rows.
We planted our garden,
Now see how it grows!

T is for trees

In the spring, buds are small,
Then leaves will unfold,
And turn colors by fall!

V is for vases
Just bursting with flowers—
Tulips and lilies—
All thanks to spring showers!

U is for umbrella
I keep one nearby.
When raindrops start falling,
It keeps me so dry!

W is for wind
That blows through my hair.
The butterflies whirl and swirl,
Playing on air!

X is in equino**X**
It falls twice a year.
The one that's in March
Means springtime is here!

Y is for yard
And there's nothing as great
As playing all day,
'Cause the sun goes down late!

Z is for zillions
Of fun things to do
So have a nice spring,
And a great summer, too!